EGG HUNT

Written by Scott Nickel
Illustrated by Mike Fentz and Lori Barker
Designed by Kenny Goetzinger and Brad Hill

Garfield created by
JIM DAVIS

Scholastic Reader — Level 1

ISBN 0-439-67211-2

12   11   10   9   8   7   6   5   4   3   2   1   5 6 7 8 9 10

Printed in the U.S.A.
First printing, March 2005

SCHOLASTIC INC.
New York   Toronto   London   Auckland   Sydney
Mexico City   New Delhi   Hong Kong   Buenos Aires

It was Easter morning.
, and

 were going on an

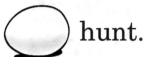 hunt.

"Let's have a contest,"

said  .

"The one who finds the most

s wins!"

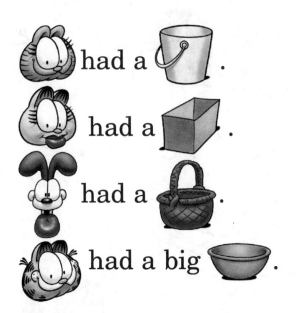

had a 🪣.

had a ▱.

had a 🧺.

had a big 🥣.

"On your mark. Get set. Go!"

said .

"May the best pet win!"

 looked in the  .

"I am the world's cutest

kitten," said .

"I will find the most s."

 looked in the  .

"I'm the nicest kitty,"

said .

"I will find the most s!"

 looked by a .

"Arf! Arf! Arf!" he barked.

 wanted to find the

most s.

"I will find the most s,

because I'm the smartest!"

said ![Garfield] .

He looked in the ![flowers] .

Then he looked by a .

A ![dog] came out and growled.

The  chased .

ran across the .

The jumped.

ducked.

The landed in the .

Splash!

Everyone met back at

the  .

 emptied his .

"I found three s and a

 ."

The hopped onto

's head.

"Ribbit!" it said.

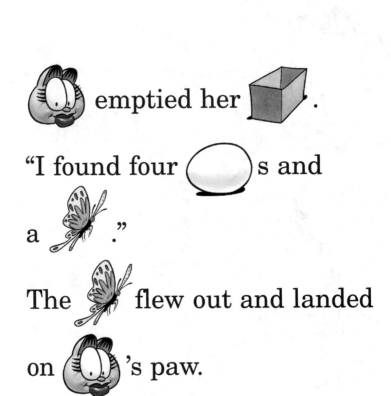

emptied her .

"I found four s and

a ."

The flew out and landed

on 's paw.

 emptied his .

"Arf! Arf!" he barked.

 found four s, two

s, and a rubber .

 did not find any s.

 emptied his .

"I found six s, including

this big blue ," said

 .

"I win, of course."

The big blue shook.

The ⬭ cracked open.

A baby 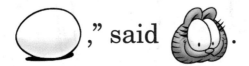 poked its head out

and chirped.

"That was a very special

⬭," said 🐱.

"Too bad it wasn't a

⬭," said 🐱.

Did you spot all of the picture clues in this Garfield Easter story?

Each picture clue is on a flash card. Ask a grown-up to cut out the flash cards. Then try reading the words on the backs of the cards. The pictures will be your clue.

Reading is fun with Garfield!

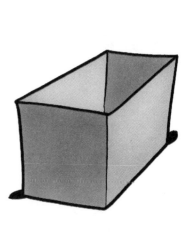

Garfield	Odie
Nermal	Arlene
box	egg

basket	bucket
grass	bowl
tree	bushes

rock	flowers
dog	frog
butterfly	doghouse

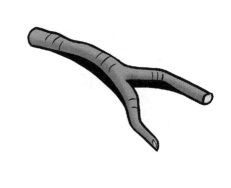

stick	birdbath
chick	mouse
chocolate	house